# WATERSHIP DOWN

# Escape to
the Hills

Other
Watership Down
fiction adventures

# Escape to the Hills

## Judy Allen

RED FOX

A Red Fox Book

Published by Random House Children's Books
20 Vauxhall Bridge Road, London SW1V 2SA

A division of The Random House Group Ltd
London  Melbourne  Sydney  Auckland
Johannesburg and agencies throughout the world

www.watershipdown.net

Illustrations by County Studio, Leicester

1 3 5 7 9 10 8 6 4 2

Printed and bound in Denmark by Nørhaven A/S

THE RANDOM HOUSE GROUP Limited Reg. No. 954009

www.randomhouse.co.uk

ISBN 0 09 940355 2

This story represents scenes from
the television series, Watership Down,
which is inspired by Richard Adams'
novel of the same name.

# *Contents*

# *The Characters of Watership Down*

## Hazel

The leader of the group, Hazel persuaded his friends to leave their old warren at Sandleford and start a new life elsewhere.

## Fiver

One of the youngest rabbits, Hazel's brother Fiver has visions of the future – a gift that sometimes causes him many problems.

## Bigwig

A former member of the Sandleford Owsla, Bigwig naturally uses force to settle any disputes and has no time for time-wasters.

## Pipkin

The youngest and most vulnerable rabbit, Pipkin is innocent, sweet and adventurous, and a well-loved friend to all the group.

# Blackberry

An intelligent doe, Blackberry is a great problem solver and at times of crisis, she is the calm voice of reason.

# Hawkbit

Hawkbit is always ready to look on the glum side, but when the going gets tough, his loyalty to the group shines through.

# Dandelion

Talker, joker and storyteller, Dandelion is always ready to celebrate the heroic deeds of the warren and El-Arah.

# Kehaar

A newcomer to the group, Kehaar thinks he's much cleverer than the rabbits, but infact he can't manage without them.

# Hannah

A fearless fieldmouse, Hannah often tends to forget her size and has no problem trading insults with bigger animals.

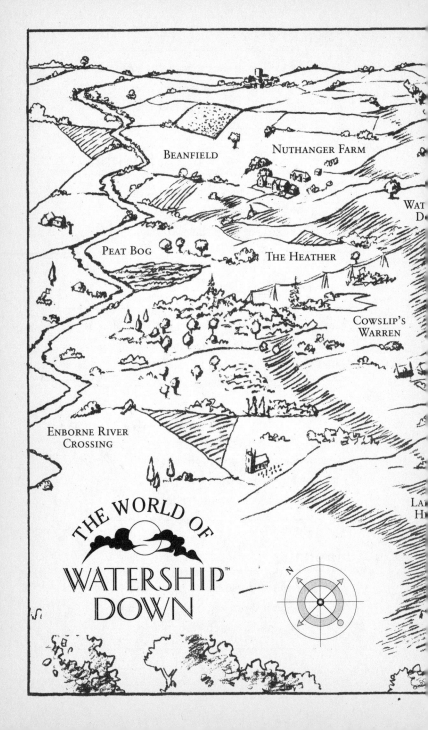

BEANFIELD

NUTHANGER FARM

WAT
D

PEAT BOG

THE HEATHER

COWSLIP'S
WARREN

ENBORNE RIVER
CROSSING

LA
H

THE WORLD OF

WATERSHIP™
DOWN

N

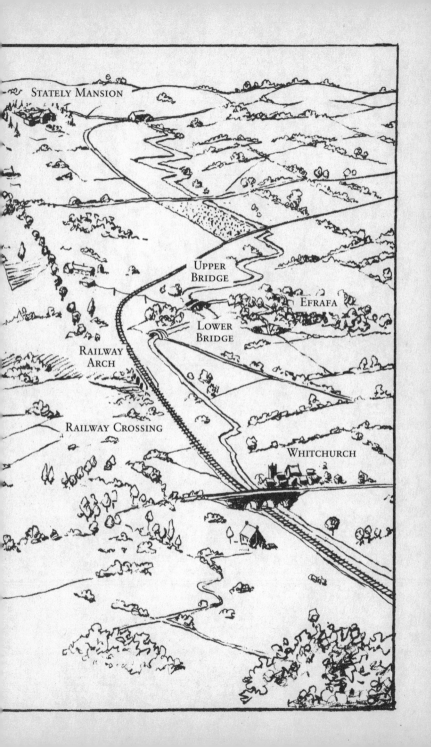

## CHAPTER ONE

# Fiver's Warning

Hazel sat apart from the other rabbits, on a mound which gave him a good view. His younger brother, Fiver, was beside him.

They were in a wide clearing in the woods. The gap in the trees had allowed sweet grass to grow and Blackberry, the only doe, was

nibbling calmly. Hawkbit was eating,
too. Dandelion was resting. Pipkin,
the youngest, was chasing a butterfly.

Only Bigwig, the large buck,
seemed wary and alert.

They were a long way from home, and Hazel watched them anxiously. They were here because he had led them, and he had led them because of Fiver's warning.

He looked at Fiver, who was crouching low, eyes closed, ears twitching. 'What can you see?' he asked.

'High lonely hills,' said Fiver softly. 'That's where we'll find our new home.'

Overhead, a seagull let out a harsh cry, startling them all.

'What's that?' said Pipkin, eyes wide. 'Is he elil?'

'Not all birds are enemies,' said Blackberry gently. 'He's just a gull.'

'Young bucks!' said Bigwig. 'Don't know anything!'

Hawkbit hopped closer. 'As a captain of Owsla, you know everything, do you?' he said to Bigwig. 'Well I'll tell you what I know – we should never have left the warren at Sandleford. Captain Holly tried to stop us. We should have listened.'

Fiver shivered. He spoke as if in a dream. 'Darkness comes in the light of day. No future at all for those who stay.'

'He's off again,' said Dandelion. 'Seeing visions –'

He stopped as the hunting bark of a large dog echoed through the trees.

'Run!' shouted Hazel.

In a second the glade was empty.
The younger rabbits raced ahead.
Hazel and Bigwig brought up the
rear to make sure no one got left
behind.

They ran until their way was
blocked by a wide river. A distant
barking told them the dog was still
on their trail.

'Swim!' shouted Bigwig.

'I don't want to drown!' said
Hawkbit. Even so, he slid into the
water and paddled hard.

Dandelion followed, but Pipkin
held back, trembling with fear and
exhaustion.

The dog barked again, horribly
close. As Hazel turned, ready to face
it, he heard Blackberry calling from
upstream – 'Here! There's a way
across.' He and Bigwig ran towards
her, herding Pipkin and Fiver
ahead of them.

Blackberry had found a floating log. Pipkin scrambled on to it, Fiver followed, and Blackberry gave it a push just as the huge dog exploded out of the undergrowth. The log bobbed away from the bank, with the two smallest rabbits aboard. Blackberry, Hazel and Bigwig dived into the water, inches ahead of the snapping jaws.

The dog didn't follow. He had seen something the frantically swimming rabbits had not. The current was carrying the log, with Pipkin and Fiver clinging to it, slowly back towards him.

'Oh, Pipkin, I'm sorry it had

to end like this,' said Fiver, helplessly.

The log lurched and a voice gasped, 'Nothing's ending!'

Bigwig had swum back across the river. Now he kicked out strongly, pushing the log away from under the nose of the angry dog.

The others shouted encouragement and, as soon as the log was within reach, helped Pipkin and Fiver ashore.

'Well done, Bigwig!' said Hazel. 'And that was a clever trick, Blackberry. Now, let's move on.'

'We're half dead, Hazel,' said Hawkbit. 'Give us a chance.'

Hazel shook his head. 'We'll rest when we find a safe place,' he said. 'We're not safe yet.'

## CHAPTER TWO

# *Frith's Blessing*

The tired rabbits knew Hazel was right, they must keep moving. Wearily they followed until Hazel, scouting ahead, found a perfect place to rest. It was a spreading bean field, whose tall plants would hide them from all enemies. Gratefully, they lay on the sun-warmed ground.

Pipkin woke first and hopped off to explore. A flapping of wings startled him. Then a large bird landed on a fence post nearby.

'I saw you flying!' said Pipkin. 'You're a gull, aren't you?'

'Kehaar, gull from sea,' said the bird. 'You know way to sea?'

'No,' said Pipkin. 'Are you lost, too?'

At that moment he heard
Hawkbit calling. It was time to
move on again.

'Nice meeting you, Kehaar,'
said Pipkin.

Kehaar watched him hop away.

'Everybody lost,' he said sadly.
'Nobody got a home.'

Limping on, the rabbits came to a terrible place, where the earth was dark and broken and nothing grew except fierce, spikey gorse. Dark rain clouds covered the sky.

Blackberry didn't complain, but Hawkbit did, and soon Dandelion joined in.

They were tired and hungry. This place looked like the end of the world. They didn't even know where they were going.

Bigwig kept them moving, but he took Hazel aside and said, 'Are we sure Fiver's right?'

Mist drifted over them. Rain fell.
As the weary rabbits struggled on
Hazel sighed. 'We can't go back
now,' he said.

Soon, even Fiver began to lose
faith. He slipped in the mud and lay
there, shivering. 'What if my vision
was wrong?' he said miserably.
'What if I'm mad?'

But Bigwig had seen something. He pointed ahead, to a gap in the surrounding mist. In the far distance lay a line of high hills, touched by sunlight. Almost at once the mist hid them again, but it had been enough.

'Fiver's promised land!' said Hawkbit. 'It's far off, but it's real!'

The mist shifted once more and revealed a small farm, not far below. The smell of lettuces and carrots floated up to the hungry rabbits.

Bigwig wanted to head there at once, but Hazel was cautious. 'We're exhausted,' he said. 'We need our wits about us for a raid.'

'And we need food if we're going to make it to the high hills,' said Bigwig.

Blackberry, Fiver and Pipkin kept quiet. Hawkbit and Dandelion sided with Bigwig.

'At least wait until it's dark,' said Hazel.

'Fair enough,' said Bigwig.

Hazel looked thoughtfully at the

bedraggled band of rabbits. Then he brightened. 'What about a story, Dandelion?' he said.

'All right,' said Dandelion. 'Shall I tell "Frith's Blessing"?'

'Yes please!' said Pipkin, cheering up.

'Long ago,' Dandelion began,
'when Frith, the Great Sun, made the
world, all animals lived peacefully
together – fox, rabbit, weasel –
sharing the same grass.

'El-Arah, the father of all rabbits,
had many children. Soon they
covered the whole world, eating
everything.

'Frith told El-Arah he must control his people – but El-Arah refused. So Frith blessed the other animals with special gifts. To the fox and the weasel he gave claws and teeth and the desire to hunt El-Arah's people.

'When El-Arah heard this, he was afraid. He tried to hide, but Frith found him and said, "Come, El-Arah, I'll give you your blessing."

'El-Arah's hind legs grew long and strong and his ears grew long and sharp. Frith said, "Those are your gifts, El-Arah. Never again will your people cover the world because it is filled with enemies. But first they must catch you! Runner! Digger! Listener! Be cunning and full of tricks – and your people will never be destroyed."'

Dandelion paused. 'And it's true,' he said. 'We're not destroyed. We're still here.'

'Well told, Dandelion,' said Hazel.

'Right, Runners, Diggers, Listeners!' said Bigwig. 'Let's be cunning and trick Man out of some lettuce!'

## CHAPTER THREE

# *The Raid on the Farm*

Under cover of darkness, the rabbits made their way towards the farm.

The smell of food drew them to a large shed next to the farmhouse. Outside stood a stack of crates, each one brimming with fresh vegetables.

'This must be all the flayrah in

the world!' said Pipkin.

'So who's going to miss a few carrots?' said Bigwig, as they crowded round and began to eat.

They were too busy to notice that, inside the big shed, Kehaar the gull was on a raid of his own. Not for the first time, he had persuaded Hannah the fieldmouse to help him.

'We were lucky to get away with stealing the cat's fish last time,' said

Hannah. 'After this, no more!'

She led him past the big tractor,
to where the cat's bowls stood.
Kehaar saw sardines in the food
bowl, and his beak watered.

'Rotten cat's somewhere else,'
said Hannah. 'Quick.'

But the cat wasn't somewhere
else. She was perched on the tractor,
watching.

As Kehaar flipped the first fish
into his beak, she sprang.

Kehaar squawked, the cat yowled,
Hannah squealed. Startled by the

noise, the rabbits scattered – just as
Hannah hurtled out of the shed
screaming, 'Run! The cat's got
Kehaar!'

'Kehaar!' said Pipkin, horrified,
and he turned back towards the
tractor shed.

'No!' cried Hazel.

'Idiot young buck!' roared Bigwig,
and raced after him, Hazel and the
others at his heels.

'Kehaar's lost like us,' said Pipkin.
'We have to help him.'

'Not against a cat!' said Hawkbit.

The cat was slashing at the cornered gull.

'Come on, cat!' Kehaar squawked defiantly. 'I show you a fight...'

Then Hazel, Bigwig and Hawkbit charged, ramming the cat so hard

she fell into a stack of flowerpots,
which rained down all over her.

'Kehaar! Quick!' yelled Hannah.

Kehaar raced for freedom on foot,
followed by the three rabbits. The
group gathered, panting, against a
wall outside the farm.

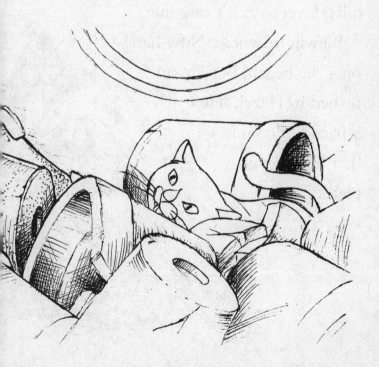

'Kehaar, are you all right?' gasped Pipkin.

'Wing hurt,' said Kehaar.

'You won't last long with a bad wing,' said Hannah.

'Come with us,' said Pipkin eagerly. 'We're going to the high hills. Fiver says it's safe there.'

Bigwig frowned. 'Now hang on –' he began, but Pipkin turned to Hazel. 'He's a friend,' he said. 'Let him come, please.'

Hazel looked thoughtful. Then he said, 'We're all newcomers. We should help each other. I think Kehaar should stay with us.'

The others didn't seem to mind, so Bigwig gave in. 'All right,' he said. 'Now let's go!'

It was a long way to the high
hills, and the sky was light by the
time Hazel led them up the last
slope. Kehaar flew low beside
them, Hannah on his back.

At last seven weary rabbits sat
near an ancient beech tree, looking
out over the lush grass of the downs.

'This is where we'll start again,'
said Hazel.

Kehaar landed awkwardly. 'Is
good place,' he said approvingly.

'Its name is Watership Down,'
said Hannah.

'Watership Down,' said Fiver
softly. 'Home.'

Some way away, a weasel rose on his haunches, sniffing a scent carried on the morning air. 'Long-ears,' he murmured to himself. 'Long-ears are back on the Down.'

CHAPTER FOUR

# *The New Burrow*

Next morning, Blackberry made an interesting discovery. In the bank under the beech tree was an old, abandoned rabbit hole. 'It isn't big enough,' she said, 'but if everyone helps with the digging...'

'Everyone?' said Bigwig. 'But bucks don't dig.'

47

'Be fair,' said Hazel. 'Blackberry's the only doe. She can't dig the whole warren by herself. We'll all have to pitch in.'

Hawkbit, Dandelion, Pipkin and Fiver looked blank. Bigwig shook his head firmly.

'If we're going to survive,' said Hazel, 'we need new ways of thinking.'

'I've had enough of new

thinking,' said Bigwig. 'You've already got us living with gulls and mice.'

'You don't like mice?' said Hannah, offended. 'Fine. Mouse gone.' And she marched away through the grass.

Hazel sighed. Then he hopped into the burrow to set an example by helping Blackberry.

The other rabbits settled to nibbling the grass.

Kehaar waddled up to Pipkin.
'Kehaar hungry,' he said. 'You help
get food?'

Readily, Pipkin followed the gull
away from the others until they
found a piece of rotted wood. Pipkin

heaved it over so Kehaar could get
at the fat grubs underneath. Then a
chilling sound came drifting through
the air. Pipkin sat bolt upright.
A strange and lonely voice was
calling on the wind – 'Bigwig.
Bigwig. Where are you?'

Frozen with fear, Pipkin didn't notice something creeping up behind him. When he turned, the weasel was almost on top of him, its teeth bared in an evil grin.

But before it could strike, Bigwig, Hazel and Hawkbit appeared out of nowhere. They charged the weasel, as they had the cat, and sent it rolling down the slope.

'I told you we shouldn't mix with gulls and mice,' said Bigwig angrily. 'That bird led Pipkin off on his own.'

'Kehaar stupid! Kehaar sorry!' said the gull miserably.

'And who saw the weasel, and came all the way back to warn us?' said Hazel. 'Hannah, the mouse.'

'True,' said Bigwig, 'but it was still that gull's fault –' Then he noticed that Pipkin was shivering with shock. 'Don't let a rotten weasel upset you,' he said gently.

'It's more than that,' said Pipkin. 'I heard a voice calling your name. What if... what if it was the Black Rabbit of Inle.'

Bigwig's eyes widened. Then he ruffled Pipkin's head. 'If he wants me, he knows where to find me,' he said casually.

The arguments about the digging went on for most of the morning. Eventually Bigwig, Hawkbit and Dandelion agreed to help, but they were not happy. Only Fiver and

Pipkin went willingly into the burrow to start work.

Hazel was sitting alone, Hannah at his side.

'It's no good having two leaders,' said the fieldmouse. 'There can only be one.'

Hazel sighed. 'Maybe it's time for Bigwig to take over,' he said.

'But you brought the rabbits to Watership Down,' said Hannah. 'That means you're the leader.'

Beyond the great beech tree, Bigwig sat upright, listening.

But he wasn't listening to Hannah or Hazel. He was listening to the far-off eerie voice, still calling his name.

## CHAPTER FIVE

# An Unexpected Visitor

Earth flew in all directions as the digging of the new warren got under way. At first the bucks weren't very good at it, but Blackberry supervised them and they worked hard. By late afternoon they had cleared out a big chamber, its high ceiling held up by the roots of the beech tree above.

While they were admiring it,
Pipkin discovered a rock-lined tunnel

that led out of the back of the chamber. Hazel squeezed into it and then backed out again. 'It's too narrow to be any use as a burrow,' he said. 'But it seems to go a long way, and the air smells fresh.'

'My uncle told me about a tunnel that goes from here to the far side of the Down,' said Hannah. 'This must be it.'

Hazel looked thoughtful. 'That weasel's a threat to us all,' he said. 'If we can make him go down this tunnel, we can block the entrance behind him.'

'Good thinking,' said Bigwig. 'And he'll come out too far off to find his way back. But how do we get him in? Ask nicely?'

'I'll make him chase me in,' said Hazel. 'Then you can block the tunnel after us.'

'But you'll be trapped in there with him!' said Hawkbit.

'I know,' said Hazel. 'But it has to be done.'

Bigwig stepped forwards. 'I'll do it,' he said. 'The Black Rabbit of Inle is coming for me anyway. I heard him calling. Pipkin heard him, too.'

Pipkin nodded.

'When the Black Rabbit comes to take you to the Other Side, you go,' said Bigwig. 'Hazel, we've had our differences, but the rabbits of Watership Down need you and your new ideas. Let me do this last thing for everyone.'

Very reluctantly, Hazel agreed.

The other rabbits were shocked at the thought of Bigwig's sacrifice, and Kehaar sobbed loudly. Bigwig took no notice. He busied himself showing them where to hide and instructing Kehaar on when to sound the alarm.

Then Hannah nudged Hazel. 'I've got a plan,' she whispered. 'Listen –'

Hawkbit was just beginning a solemn farewell speech to Bigwig, when Hazel interrupted him. 'Wait!' he said. 'It's OK! Hannah will lead the weasel into the rock tunnel. She's found a tiny crack, just big enough for her to escape afterwards.'

Bigwig didn't like the idea of giving such an important job to a mouse but, for the first time, all the other rabbits sided against him, and finally he agreed.

When the weasel returned that night, the moonlight showed him a small fieldmouse at the burrow opening. 'Mouse mouthful,' murmured the weasel. 'Long-ear later.' And he chased Hannah into the burrow.

Kehaar gave the signal and Hazel, Bigwig and Blackberry crept out of their hiding place and followed. As soon as the weasel was right inside the narrow tunnel, they raced over and heaved a rock across the opening. Seconds later, Hannah popped out of the escape-crack.

'You were wonderful, Hannah!' said Hazel.

'I suppose mice and gulls aren't completely useless,' said Bigwig, grudgingly.

Outside, Fiver and Pipkin waited
anxiously with Hawkbit, Dandelion
and Kehaar. But no sooner had the
others come out of the burrow to tell
them the trap had worked than the
strange voice called again, closer
this time – 'Bigwig –
where are you?'

'The Black Rabbit of Inle,' whispered Hawkbit.

Bigwig nodded. 'I have to go now,' he said solemnly, and he walked away from them into the darkness.

Hazel and Fiver looked at each other – then hurried to catch up with him.

'Go back,' said Bigwig, 'or the Black Rabbit will take you, too.'

'We won't let you face him alone,' said Hazel.

The voice called Bigwig's name once more, very close now. A dark rabbit-shape loomed in front of them. As they hesitated, the figure ran to Bigwig and collapsed at his feet.

'By Frith!' said Hazel. 'It's Captain Holly.'

Holly was a dreadful sight – dirty, exhausted, wounded. 'I've been searching...' he wailed. 'Fiver, you were right – we should all have left – Sandleford Warren is gone. Destroyed!'

'Did anyone else get out?' said Fiver, his eyes wide.

'Pimpernel. He was too weak to walk far. I left him at another warren –'

Holly was shaking all over.

'It's all right,' said Bigwig, helping him up. 'You're safe now.'

'Oh, Hazel, I was right,' said Fiver, shocked. 'Sandleford's gone and we're all alone. What do we do?'

'What our ancestors did before us,' said Hazel. 'We start again.'

# Glossary

**Buck**      A male rabbit

**Doe**      A female rabbit

**Efrafa**      The name of General
Woundwort's warren

**El-Arah**      The shortened name of the
rabbit hero, El-ahrairah. The
many stories of El-Arah are
an inspiration to all rabbits

**Elil**      Enemies of rabbits; like foxes,
hawks and weasels

**Flayrah**      Good food; like carrots,
cabbages and lettuces

**Frith**      The sun; a god to the rabbits

**Frithmas**     The rabbits' Christmas
celebration; it is celebrated
with a great feast

**Inle**     The moon; when it is time
for a rabbit to die, the Black
Rabbit of Inle comes to
fetch him

**Owsla**     A group of strong brave
rabbits who are trained to
defend the warren

**Silflay**     Eating outside the warren;
usually at dawn or dusk

**Warren**     The network of burrows
where rabbits live

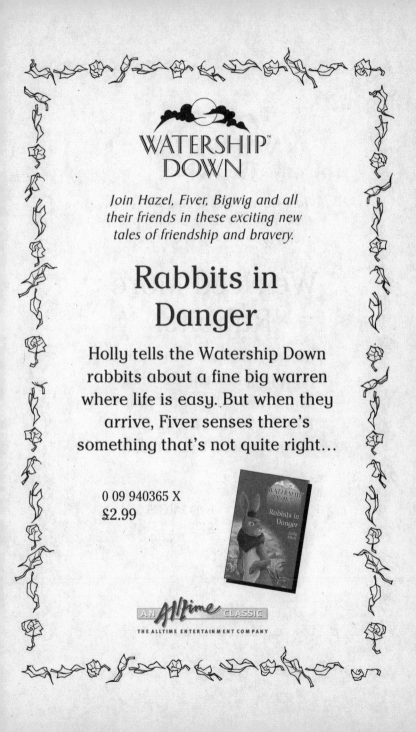

# WATERSHIP DOWN

*Join Hazel, Fiver, Bigwig and all their friends in these exciting new tales of friendship and bravery.*

# Rabbits in Danger

Holly tells the Watership Down rabbits about a fine big warren where life is easy. But when they arrive, Fiver senses there's something that's not quite right...

0 09 940365 X
£2.99

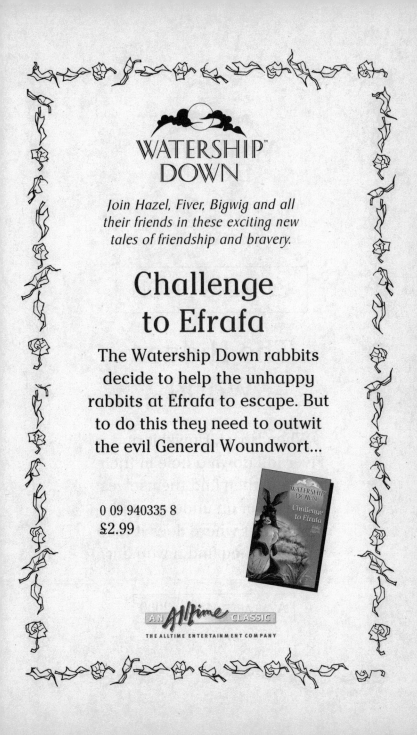

# WATERSHIP DOWN

*Join Hazel, Fiver, Bigwig and all their friends in these exciting new tales of friendship and bravery.*

## COMING SOON

# The Hidden World

When Hazel, Hawkbit and Fiver fall down a hole in their warren, they find themselves buried in an underground tunnel. But where does it lead and can they find a way out?

AVAILABLE MARCH 2000

# WATERSHIP DOWN

*Join Hazel, Fiver, Bigwig and all their friends in these exciting new tales of friendship and bravery.*

## COMING SOON

# Friend and Foe

The threat from Efrafa is growing all the time. So when Hazel finds the captain of their Owsla wounded, he tries to make friends with him and bring him round to their way of thinking.

AVAILABLE MARCH 2000